EXTREME

Find it FAST

Find the Verse You're Looking For

THOMAS NELSON PUBLISHERS

Copyright © 2002 by Thomas Nelson, Inc.

All rights reserved. Written permission must be secured from the publisher to use or reproduce any part of this book, except for brief quotations in critical reviews or articles.

Published in Nashville, Tennessee by Thomas Nelson, Inc.

Library of Congress Cataloging-in-Publication Data
Available from Library of Congress

Extreme Find it Fast
ISBN: 0-7852-4766-1

Printed in the United States of America
1 2 3 4 5—04 03 02 01

Topics

Advice
1 Samuel 25:32-34
Job 2:9
Psalm 1:1
Psalm 33:11
Acts 5:34-41

Angels
Psalm 148:2, 5
Acts 27:23-24
Hebrews 1:14
Hebrews 12:22

Beatitudes
Matthew 5:3-12
Luke 6:20-22

Believe
Acts 8:37
Acts 13:39
Romans 1:16
Romans 4:5
Romans 9:33
Hebrews 11:6
1 John 3:23
1 John 5:13

Bible
Psalm 119:160
Proverbs 30:5
1 Thessalonians 2:13
2 Timothy 3:16
Hebrews 4:12
1 Peter 4:11

Born Again
John 3:3-8
Romans 6:4-11
2 Corinthians 5:17
1 John 5:1

Boyfriend
1 Samuel 16:7
Romans 13:13-14
2 Corinthians 6:14
2 Corinthians 10:7

Bragging
Proverbs 27:1-2
Romans 11:17-21
Ephesians 2:9

Bummed
Numbers 11:10-15
2 Samuel 17:23
1 Kings 19:4
Psalm 16
Psalm 55:12
Psalm 62:1-8
Isaiah 61:1-4
Jeremiah 15:10-21
Jeremiah 20:7-8
Mark 6:31
Luke 21:28

Cash
Genesis 31:15
Deuteronomy 14:22-26
Matthew 25:27

Cocky (See Stuck Up)

Comfort
Romans 15:4
2 Corinthians 1:3-4
2 Corinthians 2:7
1 Thessalonians 4:18

Communion
Matthew 26:26-29
Luke 22:19-20

John 6:26-58
1 Corinthians 10:16
1 Corinthians 11:20-26

Compassion
Zechariah 7:9
Colossians 3:12
Jude 22

Confession
Psalm 32:1-5
Psalm 51:12-19
Proverbs 28:13
James 5:16
1 John 1:9-10

Confidence
Habakkuk 3:17-19
Acts 27:22-25
Philippians 1:6, 25
2 Timothy 1:12

Contentment
Psalm 145:7-21
Habakkuk 3:17-19
1 Timothy 6:6-8
Hebrews 13:5

Control
Proverbs 16:32
Galatians 5:22-23
1 Peter 2:11
2 Peter 1:6

Counseling
Psalm 1:1
Psalm 119:24
Proverbs 11:14
Proverbs 15:22

Courage
Joshua 1:5-7
Judges 7:7-23
Judges 16:26
1 Samuel 17:46
Acts 3:12-26

Cross
Matthew 27:32
1 Corinthians 1:17-18
Galatians 4:4

Curfew
Proverbs 4:14-19
Ephesians 5:10-13
John 3:20-21
Romans 13:12
1 John 1:5-6

Cussing
Exodus 20:7
Job 2:9
Ephesians 5:3-7
James 5:12

Dad
Genesis 37:4;
Genesis 50:16
Proverbs 1:8
Hosea 11:3
Matthew 7:8-11
1 Thessalonians 2:11

Death
Psalm 23:4
Ecclesiastes 9:10
Romans 5:12
1 Corinthians 13:12
Philippians 1:21
Hebrews 9:27

Demons
Matthew 8:29-33
Matthew 12:24-30

Luke 10:17-18
1 Timothy 4:1

Depressed (See Bummed)

Devos

Psalm 5:1-3
Psalm 119:147
1 Thessalonians 3:10
1 Timothy 5:5

Discipleship

Matthew 12:49-50
Matthew 16:25
John 8:12
John 12:26
John 16:13

Discretion

Genesis 41:33, 39
Psalm 112:5
Proverbs 2:11
Proverbs 11:22
Isaiah 28:26
Titus 2:5

Do Over

Psalm 51:10
Isaiah 41:4
Romans 12:2
2 Corinthians 4:16
Colossians 3:10

Do Unto Others

Matthew 7:12
Luke 6:31

Doubt

Genesis 3:4
Judges 6:36-40
Luke 1:18-20
Luke 16: 27-31
John 7:17
Acts 17:11-12

Encouragement

Joshua 1:1-9
2 Kings 6:15-17
Nehemiah 4:17-23
Esther 4:13-16
Matthew 28:19-20
Acts 4:36-37

Endurance

Matthew 10:22
2 Timothy 2:3, 10
Hebrews 10:32-33
James 1:12

Envy

Proverbs 27:4
Galatians 5:21
1 Timothy 6:4

Eternal Life

John 10:28-29
John 12:50
John 17:3
Romans 6:23
2 Timothy 1:1, 10

Faith

Luke 17:5
John 11:21-2
Acts 15:7
Romans 4:20-24
Romans 10:9-10
1 Corinthians 15:16
Hebrews 11:1-2

Fasting

2 Samuel 12:16
Nehemiah 1:4

Nehemiah 9:1-2
Esther 4:16
Psalm 35:13
Daniel 6:18-20
Zechariah 7:5-7
Matthew 6:16-18
Luke 2:37

Fate

Job 11:7-9
Psalm 75:6-7
Psalm 103:19
Psalm 145:17
Isaiah 50:2-3
Daniel 4:35

Fear

Psalm 19:9
Jeremiah 10:7
Matthew 28:4
2 Corinthians 11:3
Hebrews 11:7

Fights

Genesis 13:7-11
Proverbs 10:12
Proverbs 15:18
Proverbs 17:1, 19
1 Timothy 6:4

Forgiveness

Matthew 18:21-22
Luke 17:3-4
2 Corinthians 2:7-10
Ephesians 4:32
James 5:15-16

Freedom

Psalm 119:45
2 Corinthians 3:17
Galatians 2:4-5
Galatians 5:13
James 1:25

Friends

1 Samuel 18:1-3
1 Samuel 20:17
Proverbs 17:17
Proverbs 18:24
Proverbs 27:6-10
John 15:13

Fruit of the Spirit

Galatians 5:22-23

Gay

Leviticus 18:22
Leviticus 20:13
I Kings 14:24
Romans 1:24-27

Gentleness

2 Samuel 22:36
Colossians 3:12
1 Timothy 6:11
1 Peter 3:1-4

Giggle

Job 5:22
Psalm 59:8
Psalm 126:2

Girlfriend

1 Samuel 16:7
Romans 13:13-14
2 Corinthians 6:14
2 Corinthians 10:7

Glory

Romans 5:3
Romans 8:18
2 Corinthians 3:18
Galatians 6:14
Colossians 1:27

Topics

Godliness
1 Timothy 4:7-8
1 Timothy 6:5-11
Titus 2:12

Goodness
Exodus 34:6
Psalm 52:1
Psalm 145:7
Jeremiah 31:14
Galatians 5:22-23
Ephesians 5:9

Grace
Acts 4:33
Acts 15:11
Romans 5:15-20
Ephesians 4:29
1 Timothy 1:12-16
1 Peter 3:7
2 Peter 3:18

Grief
Job 1:18-21
Isaiah 25:8
Isaiah 35:10
Isaiah 51:11
John 11:23-28, 41-44
1 Thessalonians 4:13-18
Revelation 21:4

Guilt
Isaiah 64:6
Romans 5:12-14
Galatians 3:22

Guts
Proverbs 28:1
Acts 9:27-29
Ephesians 6:19
Philippians 1:14
Hebrews 4:16
1 John 4:17

Hangin' Out
Psalm 133:1-3
Acts 2:42
Philippians 2:1
Philippians 3:10
1 Peter 3:8
1 John 1:3

Happy
Proverbs 15:13
Zechariah 9:16-17
John 16:33

Hard Working
Deuteronomy 4:9
Deuteronomy 6:17
Proverbs 4:23
Proverbs 10:4
2 Peter 1:5-10

Healing
Genesis 20:17-18
Jeremiah 17:14
Ezekiel 47:8-11
Malachi 4:2
Matthew 4:24

Heaven
1 Kings 8:30
Matthew 23:34, 37
Luke 20:36
Acts 7:55-56
2 Corinthians 12:4
Hebrews 9:12, 24
Revelation 7:17
Revelation 21:4

Hell
Matthew 25:41, 46
2 Thessalonians 1:9

Helping

Acts 20:28, 35
1 Corinthians 12:28
1 Thessalonians 5:14

Holiness

Romans 8:29
1 Corinthians 3:16-17
Ephesians 4:24
1 Thessalonians 4:7

Holy Spirit

Matthew 28:19
John 3:3, 8
John 14:16, 26
Romans 8:26
Romans 15:16
1 Corinthians 12:3-11
Hebrews 10:15
2 Timothy 3:16

Homework

Acts 17:11
2 Timothy 2:15
2 Timothy 3:14

Honesty

Psalm 1:1-3
Isaiah 33:13-17
Luke 8:15
2 Corinthians 13:7
1 Peter 2:12

Honor

1 Samuel 2:30
Proverbs 3:16
Proverbs 20:3
John 12:26
Ephesians 6:2
1 Timothy 1:17

Hope

1 Corinthians 13:13
2 Corinthians 1:7
Titus 2:13
Hebrews 6:19
1 Peter 1:3

Humility

1 Kings 3:11-14
2 Chronicles 7:14-15
Proverbs 3:34
Proverbs 22:4
Isaiah 57:15
Matthew 18:4
James 4:10

Husbands

Proverbs 5:18-19
Malachi 2:14-15
Romans 7:2-3
Ephesians 5:25-33
1 Timothy 5:8

Immanuel

Isaiah 7:14
Matthew 1:23

Impatience

Psalm 13
Psalm 40:1-5
Ecclesiastes 3:1-15
Hebrews 6:13-20

Insecurity

Deuteronomy 31:1-8
Psalm 108
Philippians 4:10-20
1 John 3:19-24

Integrity

Genesis 20:3-10

Numbers 16:15
2 Corinthians 4:2
2 Corinthians 7:2

Jealousy
Genesis 37:3-11
Proverbs 6:34-35
Song of Solomon 8:6
2 Corinthians 11:2
James 3:13-18

Joy
Isaiah 51:11
Jeremiah 15:16
Acts 8:8
2 Corinthians 8:2
1 Peter 1:8
1 John 1:4

Judgment
2 Chronicles 7:19-22
2 Chronicles 36:16-17
Romans 1:18-32

Justification
Romans 4:25
Romans 5:17-21
James 2:18

Kids
Psalm 127:3
Proverbs 22:6
Matthew 18:1-5
Romans 8:16-17
1 Thessalonians 2:7

Kill
Exodus 20:13
Matthew 15:19
Matthew 5:21-22
Galatians 5:19

Kindness
Nehemiah 9:17
Isaiah 54:8, 10
Acts 28:2
2 Corinthians 6:6
Ephesians 2:7

Knowledge
Proverbs 8:10
Proverbs 24:5
Isaiah 5:13
1 Corinthians 8:1
Philippians 1:9
2 Peter 3:18

Laziness
Proverbs 6:9-11
Proverbs 18:9
Proverbs 19:15, 24
Matthew 25:26-30
Ephesians 5:16
2 Thessalonians 3:10-12

Lesbian (See Gay)

Loneliness
Psalm 22
Psalm 42
John 14:15-31
2 Timothy 4:16

Lord's Prayer
Matthew 6:9-13

Love
Matthew 22:37-38
Mark 12:31-33
1 Corinthians 13:1-13
1 John 4:17-19

Loyalty
Luke 16:13

Acts 25:7-11
Romans 13:1-2

Luck
Genesis 12:1-2
Psalm 1:1-6
Matthew 3:10-12
Matthew 6:26-33
Acts 14:17
Romans 8:30

Marriage
Genesis 2:18-24
Matthew 19:5-6
John 2:1-11
Ephesians 5:21-33
Hebrews 13:4

Meditation
Psalm 49:3
Psalm 63:5-6
Psalm 119:99
1 Timothy 4:15

Mercy
Psalm 25:6
Isaiah 54:7
Isaiah 55:3
Lamentations 3:22-23
Romans 12:8
Titus 3:5
Hebrews 4:16
1 Peter 1:3

Messiah
Psalm 2:6-12
Psalm 68:18
Psalm 72:10-15
Isaiah 7:14
Matthew 2:1-11
Ephesians 4:8-10
Philippians 2:9-10

Mom
Genesis 3:16
Genesis 25:21
Psalm 113:9
John 16:21

Money Management
Psalm 24:1-2
Matthew 25:14-15
Luke 12:42
Romans 16:23

Neighbor
Jeremiah 31:34
Luke 10:29, 37
Romans 13:9-10
Ephesians 4:25

Obedience
Acts 5:36-37
Romans 6:17
2 Corinthians 2:4
2 Corinthians 7:15

Occult
Exodus 22:18
Deuteronomy 18:10-14
Jeremiah 27:9
Acts 19:18-20

Overcomer
2 Peter 2:19-20
Revelation 2:7, 11, 17, 26; 3:5, 12, 21

Pain
Job 33:19
Psalm 25:17-18
Jeremiah 4:19

Romans 8:22
Revelation 12:2

Parenting
Exodus 20:12
Leviticus 19:3
Deuteronomy 6:6-7
1 Samuel 2:27-36
1 Kings 15:26
2 Corinthians 12:14
Ephesians 6:1
Hebrews 11:23

Party
Joshua 6:17-25
Luke 19:5-6
Romans 12:13
1 Timothy 3:2

Passion
Isaiah 9:7
Isaiah 63:15
John 2:15-17
Romans 15:18-25
2 Corinthians 7:11

Passover
Exodus 12:3-28
1 Corinthians 5:7
1 Peter 1:19

Patience
Luke 8:15
Romans 2:7
Romans 8:25
Colossians 1:12
Titus 2:2
James 1:3
James 5:7-8

Peace
Psalm 29:11
Matthew 5:9
John 14:27
Romans 5:1
2 Corinthians 13:11
Galatians 5:22
Philippians 4:7
2 Timothy 2:22

Persecution
Matthew 5:12
Matthew 5:44
Matthew 10:23
1 Corinthians 4:12
1 Peter 4:16

Perseverance
Matthew 10:22
John 15:4-8
Galatians 6:9
Ephesians 4:15
2 Timothy 1:12

Power
Mark 9:1
Romans 1:16
1 Corinthians 1:24
1 Corinthians 2:4-5
Ephesians 1:19
Hebrews 4:12

Praise
1 Chronicles 29:13
Psalm 35:28
Psalm 71:6
Psalm 72:15
Psalm 139:14
Psalm 146:2

Prayer
Genesis 18:23-33

Genesis 24:12-15
Exodus 32: 31-32
Numbers 27:15-23
Daniel 4:34-35
Matthew 6:6
Matthew 18:20
John 17:1-26
Acts 7:60
Acts 10:2, 30
1 Corinthians 14:14-17
Philippians 4:6
Colossians 1:9-12
1 Timothy 2:1-3
James 5:15
1 John 1:9

Pride (See Stuck Up)

Protection

Psalm 121:3-8
Joshua 1:5
1 Corinthians 10:13
2 Corinthians 12:9-10
2 Thessalonians 3:3

Psyched

Psalm 21:1
Psalm 51:8
Psalm 63:7
Psalm 106:5
Isaiah 51:3, 11
Habakkuk 3:18
Luke 10:20
Luke 15:32
John 20:20

Purity

Psalm 24:4
Zephaniah 3:9
1 Timothy 1:5, 15
1 Timothy 3:9
Hebrews 10:22
James 1:27
2 Peter 3:1

Reading the Bible

2 Kings 22:8-20
Psalm 119:105
Acts 17:10-11
2 Timothy 3:16-17

Rejection

Hosea 4:6
Luke 4:16-30
John 15:18
Ephesians 1:3-14
1 Peter 2:1-10

Respect

2 Kings 13:23
Psalm 40:4
Psalm 138:6
1 Samuel 2:30
1 Peter 1:17
Proverbs 3:16
Proverbs 20:3
John 12:26
Ephesians 6:2
1 Timothy 1:17

Resurrection

Matthew 22:28-29
John 11:23-44
Acts 24:14-15
Acts 26:23
1 Corinthians 6:14
1 Corinthians 15:42-55

Revenge

Jeremiah 11:20-23

Jeremiah 46:9-10
Ezekiel 25:12-17
Hebrews 10:30

Revival

Judges 15:9
2 Chronicles 7:14
Isaiah 57:15

Right and Wrong

John 8:3-5
2 Corinthians 5:17
Galatians 5:22-23
Hebrews 8:10

Righteousness

Isaiah 61:10
Jeremiah 33:16
Matthew 25:37, 46
John 17:25
1 John 2:1

Risky (See Boldness)

Safety

Deuteronomy 33:12
Psalm 4:8
Philippians 3:1

Salvation

Acts 4:12
Romans 5:8
1 Corinthians 1:18
Ephesians 2:5-8
Philippians 2:12
1 Thessalonians 5:9
Titus 3:5

Sanctification

John 17:17, 19
1 Thessalonians 5:23
1 Timothy 4:4-5
Hebrews 2:12
Hebrews 9:14
1 Peter 1:2

Satan

Job 2:2-4
Matthew 4:6
Matthew 12:24
Matthew 13:19
Luke 13:16
2 Corinthians 2:11
2 Corinthians 11:14
1 Peter 5:8
Revelation 12:10

Seeking

Proverbs 2:4
Matthew 6:33
2 Corinthians 12:14
Hebrews 11:14
1 Peter 3:11

Selfishness

Romans 13:13-14
Galatians 5:16-17
Philippians 2:21
2 Timothy 3:2

Sermon on the Mount

Matthew 5:1–7:27

Servant

Genesis 9:25
Joshua 1:2
1 Samuel 3:9
Isaiah 42:1
Acts 2:18
2 Timothy 2:24
Revelation 22:3

Shepherd

Psalm 78:52-53
Isaiah 40:11
John 10:6, 11, 14
Hebrews 13:20
1 Peter 5:2, 4

Shield

2 Chronicles 14:8
Psalm 5:12
Psalm 18:35
Psalm 33:20
Psalm 91:4
Ephesians 6:6

Show Off (See Bragging)

Sin

Isaiah 44:22
Jeremiah 31:34
Matthew 15:19-20
Romans 3:23
Romans 5:12, 16
Romans 14:23
1 Corinthians 15:3
2 Corinthians 5:21
1 Timothy 5:24

Sincerity

John 4:23-24
2 Corinthians 1:12
2 Corinthians 8:8, 24
1 Peter 2:2

Singing

Exodus 15:1, 21
Psalm 147:7
1 Corinthians 14:15
Ephesians 5:19
James 5:13
Revelation 5:9

Smarts

1 Kings 3:9-14
Psalm 119:18
1 Corinthians 2:14
2 Peter 1:1
1 John 4:1-6

Spiritual Gifts

Romans 12:6-8
1 Corinthians 12:4-30
Ephesians 3:2-10

Stealing

Exodus 20:15
Matthew 6:19
Romans 13:9
Ephesians 4:28

Stick Around

John 15:4-7
1 Corinthians 3:14
1 Peter 1:23
2 John 2

Strength

Ecclesiastes 7:19
Isaiah 40:31
Isaiah 41:10
Luke 22:32
2 Corinthians 12:9
Ephesians 3:16
2 Timothy 4:17

Stressed Out

Psalm 63:1-8
Mark 4:35-41
Philippians 4:4-6
Hebrews 13:5
1 John 4:13-18

Stoked (See Psyched)

Stuck Up
Psalm 40:4
Psalm 119:21
Proverbs 8:13
Proverbs 21:24
Isaiah 13:11
Jeremiah 48:29
James 4:6

Suicidal (See Bummed)

Suffering
Romans 8:18
1 Corinthians 12:26
2 Corinthians 1:5-7
Philippians 1:29
Hebrews 5:8
1 Peter 3:18
1 Peter 4:13

Sweet
Genesis 33:13
1 Samuel 30:11-15
Psalm 22:26
Psalm 25:9
Psalm 37:11
Matthew 5:5
Luke 10:33-36
Luke 15:11-24

Temptation
Matthew 4:7
Matthew 6:13
Hebrews 4:15
James 1:13

Ten Commandments
Exodus 20:1-17
Exodus 32:16

Tenderness
Genesis 33:13
1 Samuel 30:11-15
Luke 10:33-36
Luke 15:11-24

Thankfulness
Psalm 116:17
Daniel 2:23
John 11:41
Ephesians 1:16
Ephesians 5:20
Philippians 1:3
1 Thessalonians 2:13

Ticked Off
Proverbs 14:17
Matthew 5:21-24
Ephesians 4:26, 31
James 1:19-21

Tithing
Leviticus 27:30-33
Deuteronomy 14:22-29
Malachi 3:7-12

Tough Life
Numbers 14:7, 9
Psalm 139:6, 14
Mark 11:23-24
2 Peter 3:16
Hebrews 7:1-6

Trash Talking
Leviticus 19:6
Psalm 52:2
Proverbs 10:18
Proverbs 11:9
Proverbs 16:27-30
Proverbs 20:19

Matthew 5:11-12
Ephesians 4:31
1 Timothy 5:13
Titus 3:1-2

Trust

Psalm 33:21
Psalm 119:42
Proverbs 3:5-6
Jeremiah 17:5
Matthew 12:17-21

Truth

Psalm 119:142-160
John 14:6, 17
John 17:17, 19
Galatians 2:5, 14
Ephesians 4:15
1 Peter 1:22

Tunes

Isaiah 5:12
Ephesians 5:19
Colossians 3:16

Walk Away From

1 Samuel 7:3
Joel 3:5-8
Acts 9:1-20
Acts 9:35
Acts 15:3

Will of God

Matthew 6:10
Romans 2:18
Romans 12:2
1 Timothy 2:4
2 Peter 3:9

Win

Psalm 110:1-7
Acts 2:29-36
Philippians 4:13
Revelation 19:11-21

Wisdom

Exodus 31:3
Deuteronomy 4:6
Proverbs 3:13
Proverbs 4:5-10
Proverbs 5:1-6
Proverbs 10:31
Ecclesiastes 7:12-19
Isaiah 43:6

Wives

Proverbs 31:10
Ephesians 5:33
Titus 2:4-5
1 Peter 3:5-6

Worn Out

Psalm 4:4-8
Matthew 11:25-30
2 Thessalonians 3:6

Worry

Psalm 37:1-5
Matthew 6:24-34
Matthew 10:26-31
Philippians 4:6
1 Peter 5:6-7

Worship

1 Chronicles 16:29
John 4:20-24
Hebrews 1:6
Revelation 4:10-11